MUTILATED MONKEY MEAT

MUTILATED MONKEY MEAT

TODD STRASSER

AN
APPLE
PAPERBACK

SCHOLASTIC INC.
New York Toronto London Auckland Sydney

To a couple of cool campers,
Julia and Madeline Bloch.

No part of this publication may be reproduced in whole or in part, or stored in a retrieval system, or transmitted in any form or by any means, electronic, mechanical, photocopying, recording, or otherwise, without written permission of the publisher. For information regarding permission, write to Scholastic Inc., 555 Broadway, New York, NY 10012.

ISBN 0-590-74262-0

Copyright © 1997 by Todd Strasser. All rights reserved. Published by Scholastic Inc. APPLE PAPERBACKS and logo are trademarks and/or registered trademarks of Scholastic Inc.

12 11 10 9 8 7 6 5 4 3 2   7 8 9/9 0 1 2/0

Printed in the U.S.A.   40
First Scholastic printing, June 1997

CHAPTER

"Hey, Lucas, you hear about the corpse who ran the hundred-yard dash?" my friend Justin asked as he unwrapped a Snickers bar. A big vat of tomato sauce bubbled on the industrial-size stove behind him.

"Nope," I said as I hacked up two dozen heads of lettuce.

"He finished dead last," he said. "Get it? *Dead* last!"

I rolled my eyes and wiped the sweat off my forehead. Justin and I were wearing white aprons. We were assistant cooks at Camp Run-a-Muck.

Too bad we didn't know how to cook.

Justin bit into the candy bar, then wiped the sweat off his forehead with the back of his hand. He's average height like me, with straight brown hair he parts in the middle. He was thirteen and I was fourteen. The minimum age for working was sixteen. But

1

no one at Camp Run-a-Muck seemed to care.

"You hear about the food fight last night?" Justin asked. "They were throwing whole plates of baked beans like Frisbees. It looked like a lot of fun."

"Can't blame them," I said, gesturing to the soggy spaghetti and rock-hard meatballs we were preparing for lunch. "This stuff isn't good for anything except throwing."

Justin took another bite of his candy bar. "You're right. I don't know what I'd do without candy. Probably starve. That reminds me. You hear about the cannibal who came home late for dinner?"

I shook my head.

"His wife gave him the cold shoulder," Justin said. "Get it?"

"Yes, Justin." I looked up at the ceiling of the Camp Run-a-Muck kitchen. Hanging above us were long yellow strips of flypaper with hundreds of flies stuck to them. Most of the flies were dead. Terry Thomas, the camp's chief cook, was up on a ladder, picking the live ones off the sticky tape. He pulled off their wings and put them in a glass jar.

Terry was a tall black guy with a thing about flies.

"Don't you ever have enough flies?" I asked.

"I did," Terry growled, "until you guys stole 'em and covered them with chocolate."

The week before, Justin and I had fed chocolate-covered flies and a hamburger made of gopher guts to

2

a creep named Brad Schmook because he was a snitch.

Up on the ladder, Terry plucked the wings off another fly and dropped it into the jar.

"Hey, Terry," Justin said. "What do you call a fly with no wings?"

"Don't know," Terry replied.

"A walk," Justin said. "Get it?"

Terry and I glanced at each other and shook our heads. Neither of us laughed.

"They call it a fly because it flies," Justin tried to explain. "But a fly with no wings can't fly, it can only walk. So they call it a walk."

"Whatever you say, Justin." I started chopping lettuce heads again.

"You guys have no sense of humor," Justin complained. "I bet Bag would have laughed. Where is he, anyway? And where are the orphans?"

Bag Jammer was a six-and-a-half-foot-tall Sherpa from Tibet. He was built like Arnold Schwarzenegger and was an assistant cook like Justin and me. Bag was in charge of the six orphan Sherpas who worked on the dining hall clean-up crew.

Terry nodded toward a large walk-in refrigerator unit. The thick silver door was slightly ajar. Inside, Bag was talking to the orphan Sherpas. They were all wearing white aprons and sheepskin vests.

"What are you guys doing in here?" Justin asked them.

"We are being cool," Bag replied. "It is being too hot for us in the kitchen. In here it is being more like the climate in the mountains of Tibet."

Justin told Bag the fly joke and asked him if he thought it was funny. Bag shook his head. "I am being sorry to tell you, Justin. But this joke is not being funny."

"I bet Amanda would think it was funny," Justin sniffed.

"Go try it on her," I suggested.

"Alone?" Justin swallowed nervously. Amanda Kirby was blond and beautiful and ran the camp canteen. Justin had a crush on her, but was too chicken to talk to her alone. "I couldn't."

Just then the kitchen door swung open and a thin kid with curly brown hair walked in. It was Brad Schmook.

"Uh-oh," Justin whispered. "It's the enemy!"

Brad Schmook was the enemy because he was the personal golf caddie and gopher for Bob "The Blob" Kirby, the owner of Camp Run-a-Muck.

"Special order from Mr. Kirby," Brad said. The Blob was constantly sending him to the camp kitchen with "special orders." One of the reasons the food at Camp Run-a-Muck was so horrible was that Terry had to spend most of the food money on the fancy meals The Blob wanted for himself.

"Mr. Kirby wants a turkey club sandwich on rye toast with a side order of onion rings and a chocolate milk shake," Brad said. "And he also wants some shish kebab."

Terry looked down from the ladder and frowned. "He wants *what?*"

"Shish kebab," Brad repeated, licking his lips. "You know. Tender chunks of meat grilled on a skewer along with potatoes and onions and peppers."

"I *know* what shish kebab is," Terry grumbled. "If that's what he wants, why did he order a turkey club sandwich?"

"Guess he's really hungry today," Brad answered.

Terry shook his head. "No, Brad, I think you're really full of it today."

Justin and I shared a wink. Brad glared daggers at us.

"I don't think Mr. Kirby wants shish kebab," Terry said. "I think *you* want it. And you're trying to get me to make it by adding it on to Mr. Kirby's order."

Brad narrowed his eyes angrily. "Okay, maybe that's true. I'm totally tired of the crummy food you serve every day. I need something different and I have a craving for shish kebab. You'd better think seriously about making it. Otherwise I could make your life pretty miserable."

Terry's eyes widened with fury, and he started to climb down the ladder. "Are you threatening me? Why, I'll drop-kick your butt clear across the lake. . . ."

"I think it's time to clear out, Schmook-face," Justin said with a grin.

Brad backed away. "I'll get you guys," he muttered, then went out the kitchen door.

"**O**f course I love you, sweetheart." Later that afternoon, Terry was talking on the phone with Doris, his girlfriend. "Of course I'll come visit after work. Don't I *always*?"

If Terry wasn't pulling the wings off flies, he was usually on the phone with Doris. She worked at the girls' camp across the lake.

I wiped the sweat off my face with my apron. It was always hot in the camp kitchen. The flies buzzed around our heads, and handling so much lousy food in that heat made us feel sick.

"Hey, Terry," I said. "Think Justin and I could take a break?"

Terry put his hand over the phone and nodded. Justin and I left the kitchen and headed for the canteen.

"Help! Help!" Out in the dining hall, a screaming counselor dashed past us. On the back of his light blue Camp Run-a-Muck T-shirt, someone had painted a bull's-eye.

"Get him! Hurry! Don't let him get away!" Half a dozen laughing campers raced past, carrying bows and arrows with rubber cups on the tips.

"If you're that crazy about Amanda," I said to Justin, "why don't you just ask her for a date?"

"What if she says no?" Justin asked.

The canteen was located at the far end of the dining hall, near the front doors. It was the size of a large closet, with racks of candy and pictures of ice-cream bars. As usual, there was a long line of campers waiting to buy candy.

"Why do you think she'd say no?" I asked.

"I don't know," Justin said. "Maybe *you* could ask her for me."

"No way." I shook my head. "I'm not getting in the middle of this. Besides, you wouldn't want me to say anything in front of Brad the Cad, would you?"

"Huh?" Justin frowned. "What are you talking about?"

I nodded toward the canteen. Amanda was selling candy to campers as fast as she could. Meanwhile, Brad Schmook was leaning on the counter, talking to her.

"I don't get it," Justin whispered. "Doesn't he know she can't stand him?"

"I don't think Brad's the kind of guy who takes no for an answer," I whispered back.

Brad saw us coming and gave us a sour look. "What do you guys want?"

"What do you *think* we want, dimwit?" Justin asked back.

"Hi, guys." Amanda brushed her blond hair out of her eyes and gave us a big smile. "What can I get for you?"

"Hey!" one of the campers in line yelled. "How come they get to cut all the way to the front?"

"We're staff," Justin told him. "We only get a ten-minute break, so we don't have time to stand on line. But we'll be fast."

"I know who you guys are," said another camper. "You're the assistant cooks. You're the reason we're all waiting here. If you guys made us decent meals we wouldn't have to spend all our money on candy."

"Go tell The Blob," Justin said. "We can't make a decent meal if we don't have decent food. Maybe if he gave us more money we could buy better food."

"Forget it," said the camper. "The Blob doesn't *want* us to have good food. He wants to starve us so that we'll spend all our money on candy at the canteen. That guy must be getting rich on what he makes here."

"Hey, keep it down," said another camper in a hushed voice. "Don't let The Blob hear you. If he ever realizes what a gold mine this canteen is, he'll start charging us ten times as much for candy."

"You're right," said the first camper. "And we'd

still have to buy it. I mean, with that garbage they serve at meals, what choice would we have?"

At that moment, I happened to glance at Brad. He was no longer leaning against the counter. Instead, he was standing straight and listening closely. I couldn't tell for certain, but it seemed like he'd just gotten an idea.

CHAPTER

4

A moment later Brad hurried away. Justin started talking to Amanda. They had this little game where Amanda tried to guess the answer to his jokes.

"Here's one you'll never get," Justin said. "Why do dogs feel so hot in the summer?"

Without pausing from her candy sales, Amanda thought for a second. "That's easy. It's because they wear coats."

"You're almost right," Justin said. "But that's only *half* the answer."

Amanda frowned. "Only *half* the answer? Let's see . . . I know! A dog wears a coat *and pants*!"

Justin shook his head in amazement. "You are unreal!"

Amanda grinned.

Meanwhile I tapped my finger against my wristwatch. Our break was almost over. If Justin was going to ask Amanda to go out, he would have to do it fast.

Justin swallowed nervously, then motioned for me to move away so he could talk to Amanda in private. He spoke to her in a low voice, then left the counter.

We started back across the dining hall toward the kitchen.

"So?" I said.

"So . . . what?" Justin said.

"Did you ask her?"

"Oh, yeah." Justin was playing it cool.

"And?"

"We're going canoeing on the lake tonight," Justin said.

I felt my jaw drop. "That's great! I can't believe you finally got up the nerve to ask her!"

"Yeah." Justin grinned sheepishly. "So we'll meet her at the animal hut after work, okay?"

"You mean, *you'll* meet her at the animal hut," I corrected him.

"No, I mean, *we'll* meet her," Justin said. "You're going, too."

"What are you talking about?" I asked. "This is *your* date, not mine."

"Well, actually, it's *our* date," Justin said. "I couldn't ask her to go canoeing with me alone."

"Why not?" I asked.

"She might have said no," Justin replied.

I stared at him in disbelief. What was I going to do on a date with Justin and Amanda?

CHAPTER

5

That night after work, we walked back to the bunkhouse. It was dusk, and the campers were outside, playing tetherball, or touch football, or just hanging around talking and laughing. That was the weird thing about Camp Run-a-Muck: Even though the food was terrible, the kids still loved the camp because no one ever made them do anything they didn't want to do.

As Justin and I walked, we argued about our "date."

"You've totally wimped out this time," I said.

"Aw, come on, Lucas," Justin started to whine. "You didn't expect me to go on a date with Amanda alone."

"What am I gonna do?" I asked. "Be your chaperon?"

"No," said Justin. "Just be your normal cool self."

"Suppose things work out really well tonight between you and Amanda and it gets to the point where you don't want me around anymore," I said. "What am I supposed to do then?"

"You could bail out," Justin said.

"What are you talking about?" I sputtered. "We'll be in a canoe in the middle of the lake."

"So bring a bathing suit."

I could have murdered him. In the meantime, we reached the bunkhouse. It was a long, wooden building where the kitchen staff lived. It only had a few small windows and got to be about a hundred degrees during the day. Inside we all slept on double-decker bunk beds. The floor creaked when you walked on it, and long strips of yellow flypaper hung from the rafters.

It felt like an oven inside. Terry, the chief cook, was lying on his bunk, reading a book. Little beads of sweat dotted his forehead, and he paused every now and then to dab them off with a towel.

Not far from Terry's bunk, Bag Jammer had gathered the orphan Sherpas together for an English lesson.

"Please be repeating after me," Bag said. "I am being hot."

"I am being hot," said the orphan Sherpas.

"I am having thirst," said Bag.

"I am having thirst," said the orphan Sherpas.

"I am wanting a tall, cool glass of" — Bag paused and turned to Terry — "Excuse me for being a disturbance to you, Mr. Terry."

14

Terry looked up from his book. "What is it, Baggy?"

"I am being unable to recall the beverage that the campers drink," Bag explained.

"Booger juice," Terry said, and looked back down at his book.

"I am being thankful to you, Mr. Terry," Bag said.

"Glad to be of service, Baggy," said Terry.

Bag turned to the orphan Sherpas again. "Please be repeating after me. I am wanting a tall, cool glass of booger juice. . . ."

Justin and I showered, then changed into clean clothes.

"Ready for your big date?" I asked.

"Uh, I guess." Justin hesitated and looked nervous. "You know how to make babies, Lucas?"

I shook my head.

"First you take off the *y*, then you add *ies*," he said.

"Stop stalling, Justin," I said.

"Okay, okay, you don't have to rush me." Justin stopped by the chief cook's bunk. "How come you're reading a book, Terry?"

"Just trying to stay cool," Terry replied.

"Oh, I get it," Justin said. "Like reading is cool, right?" He bent down and read the title of the book. *"The Last Place on Earth* . . . sure, that sounds cool."

"It is cool," Terry said, dabbing his forehead with his towel. "It's about these English dudes who freeze to death trying to reach the South Pole."

15

"Then it really *is* cool!" Justin had a dumb grin on his face.

"Totally frigid," Terry said. "I keep trying to imagine I'm down there in the Antarctic with them instead of sweating to death in this oven."

"Great idea," Justin said. "Maybe you could recommend a cool book for me."

Terry thought for a moment. "How about *The Invisible Man?*"

Justin frowned. "But that's about some dude you can't see."

"Right," said Terry.

Justin started to grin. "Oh, I get it. You'd like me to disappear and leave you alone, right?"

Terry nodded slowly.

"Pretty clever," Justin said. "So, did you hear the one about the elephant who — "

Before he could tell the joke, I grabbed his arm and gave it a pull. "I said quit stalling. It's time to go."

CHAPTER

"**B**oy, that Terry sure is different," Justin said as we walked across the camp toward the animal hut. By then the sun had gone down, and it was dark. "I mean, tearing wings off flies and reading books about the South oooofff — " He stumbled over something in the dark.

"What happened?" I asked.

"I tripped," Justin said.

Lying on the ground was something that looked like a mummy. It was the size of a small camper wrapped head to foot in toilet paper.

Justin bent down and talked to it. "Anyone in there?"

"Yeah," the mummy answered. "Ricky Pulger."

Ricky Pulger was one of the younger campers.

"You want some help getting out of that stuff?" I asked.

"No, thanks," Ricky said. "My counselor says I have to stay in this all night."

"How come?" Justin asked.

"I made my bed this morning," Ricky said.

"Why'd you do that?" I asked.

"I just got tired of having a messy bed all the time," Ricky explained. "I mean, I didn't think I'd actually get *punished* for it."

"Well, this is Camp Run-a-Muck, you know," I said.

"Yeah," said Ricky. "I'll know better next time."

"Okay, Ricky," Justin said. "See you around."

"Bye, guys," Ricky said.

Justin and I continued through the dark toward the animal hut. It was on the hill behind the rec hall. As we got closer, Justin slowed down.

"Now what's the problem?" I asked.

"Nothing," Justin replied.

"How come you're walking so slow?" I asked.

"Just feel like it, I guess," Justin said.

"Don't tell me you're going to chicken out," I groaned.

"I'm not gonna chicken out," Justin said. "I'm just nervous, okay?"

"Why should you be nervous?" I asked. "Amanda already agreed to go canoeing. I'm going with you. What could go wrong?"

Just then we saw a figure ahead of us, also heading for the animal hut. As he went under the light over the front door, we saw that it was Brad Schmook.

"*That's* what could go wrong," Justin said.

CHAPTER

Brad was already inside when Justin and I stepped into the animal hut. He spun around and looked surprised.

Amanda, who was standing beside the sink, looked glad to see us.

"What are you guys doing here?" Brad asked.

"I could ask you the same question," I said.

Brad shrugged. "I, er, just came by to see how the animals are. How about you?"

"We're going canoeing with Amanda," Justin said.

Brad pressed his lips together into a hard, straight line. He didn't look happy as he walked out of the animal hut and disappeared into the dark.

Amanda let out a sigh of relief. "Thanks, guys."

"Was he bothering you?" Justin asked.

"Not exactly," Amanda said. "But he's always hanging around. He gives me the creeps. I wish he'd leave me alone."

"You ready to go canoeing?" Justin asked.

"As soon as I give Fred his formula," she said.

The walls of the animal hut were lined with glass tanks and cages filled with creatures like turtles and toads and chipmunks that had been found around the camp. Some of the other pets had been brought to camp by campers. That group included a guinea pig, a boa constrictor, some hamsters, a lot of white mice, a parrot, and an old rhesus monkey named Fred whose face had turned gray.

Amanda loved the animals. If she wasn't working in the canteen you could almost always find her with them. Justin and I watched as she dumped a couple of scoops of dark brown powder into a baby bottle, then poured in some milk and shook it up.

"Looks like cocoa," Justin said.

"Close," said Amanda. "It's a special formula of nutrients mixed with chocolate and sucrose sweetener to make it taste good."

I looked over at Fred in his cage. The thin, gray-faced monkey hardly moved. His body was covered with bare spots and sores.

"Isn't Fred a little old for a baby bottle?" I asked.

"He's lost all his teeth," Amanda explained. "And he's full of arthritis. That's why he hardly moves. He's one old monkey."

Amanda opened the cage door and handed the bottle to Fred, who brought it slowly to his lips. Meanwhile, I looked at the cages. Some of the animals

20

moved around actively and looked pretty healthy. Others hardly moved at all and looked kind of sick.

"Some of these critters don't look too well," I said.

"I know," said Amanda. "Nobody takes care of them in the winter. Some of them are so sick now, I doubt they'll last the summer."

Fred the monkey drank from his bottle for a little while and then let it fall to the floor of the cage.

"Isn't that sad?" Amanda said. "Last year he could finish the whole bottle. This year he's so feeble, he can hardly finish half of it."

"I guess he's probably not gonna last much longer, huh?" Justin said.

Amanda's eyes grew misty. For a second I thought a tear was going to roll down her cheek.

"Well, er, I guess we'd better get going," I said.

Amanda nodded and blinked back the tears. "Yes, I think we'd better."

CHAPTER

We walked down to the waterfront. Some counselors were over by the diving area with a big crowd of campers. One of the counselors was using a stick to force a blindfolded camper out to the end of a diving board.

I noticed Ralphie, the camp's barf champion, in the crowd and asked him what was going on.

"This kid's been acting kind of strange," Ralphie said. He was a short kid with red hair and freckles. "He brushes his teeth after every meal and showers at least once a day."

"Sometimes twice," said another camper.

"It's setting a really bad example," Ralphie said. "So the counselors figured they'd loosen him up by making him walk the plank."

"He won't drown, will he?" Amanda asked.

"Naw, he's a good swimmer," Ralphie assured her. "We'd never let that happen."

We went down the dock to the canoes. Justin got into the front, and I got into the back. Amanda sat in the middle. Soon we were paddling out into the lake in the moonlight. It was a clear night, and the sky was filled with stars. The dark lake water was as smooth as glass.

"So, uh, did you hear about the guy who bought a chimpanzee at a pet store and then tried to return it?" Justin asked.

Amanda didn't say anything.

"The owner of the pet store wouldn't take the chimp," Justin said. "Because he didn't have a monkey-back guarantee."

Neither Amanda nor I said a thing. I knew Justin was trying to cheer Amanda up, but he was definitely going about it the wrong way. I finally cleared my throat and said, "I have a feeling this is the wrong night to tell monkey jokes, Justin."

"Oh," Justin said. "Gee, I'm sorry about that, Amanda."

"It's okay, Justin," Amanda said with a sniff. "Fred's an old monkey. I'm sure he's enjoyed a nice long life."

"Even if it has been in a cage," Justin said.

If he hadn't been at the other end of the canoe, I would have smacked him on the head with my paddle.

We glided quietly across the lake. It was a clear, warm night, and there was hardly a sound.

Just the soft hoot of a faraway owl.

And the distant cry of a loon.

Ahhhhhhhhhhhhhhhhhhhhhhhhhhhh! And the scream of the camper as he walked off the plank.

"Oh, my gosh!" Amanda gasped.

"It's cool, Amanda," Justin reassured her. "Remember they promised us they wouldn't let the kid drown."

"It's not that!" Amanda pointed back toward the camp. "Look! The dining hall's on fire!"

CHAPTER

9

It looked like Amanda was right. A big fire glowed in a corner of the dining hall!

"That's the corner where the canteen is!" Amanda cried.

"The candy!" Justin started to paddle like a madman. "We have to save the candy!"

Justin and I paddled as fast as we could back toward the camp. As we got closer, I could see campers holding sticks around the fire.

"They can't be roasting marshmallows while the dining hall burns, can they?" I asked.

"Hey, this is Camp Run-a-Muck," Justin gasped as he paddled. "Anything's possible. That reminds me. Did you hear about the kid who wanted twenty glasses of water before he went to bed?"

"Let me guess," Amanda said. "His room was on fire?"

"You're amazing," Justin said. "How about this.

Did you hear about the guy who went to the big fire sale?"

"Uh . . . he bought three big fires?" Amanda guessed.

"I give up," Justin moaned. "You're just too good."

A few moments later we reached the camp dock. We jumped out of the canoe and hurried toward the dining hall. By now, a big crowd of campers had gathered around the fire. They were roasting marshmallows and singing camp songs:

"Great green gobs of greasy grimy gopher guts
Mutilated monkey meat
Chopped-up birdy's feet
French-fried eyeballs rolling up and down the
    street . . .
Oops! I forgot my spoon!"

"At least they're enjoying themselves," Justin said as we ran toward them.

"But why isn't anyone trying to put out the fire?" Amanda asked.

Suddenly I stopped and pointed. "That's why! The dining hall's not on fire. Someone started this fire right next to it."

"It's too close," Justin said.

I noticed Ralphie, eating a roasted marshmallow.

"Hey, Ralphie," I said. "You know who started this fire?"

He shook his head. "We found it burning, so we figured we'd roast some marshmallows."

"Well, at least the canteen isn't on fire," Justin said. "And, actually, the fire is dying down."

He was right. The flames were slowly getting lower and being replaced by smoke. As the campers stopped singing, we heard other sounds — an alarm ringing inside the dining hall. And the hissing sound of water spraying.

"It's the dining hall sprinkler system," Amanda said. "The heat from the fire must have set it off."

"We'd better go see," I said.

Justin, Amanda, and I headed for the entrance to the dining hall. I pulled open the door, but inside, the bulbous body of Bob "The Blob" Kirby blocked our path.

The camp owner glowered at us. "Where do you think you're going?"

CHAPTER

10

"We heard the alarm, Uncle Bob," Amanda explained. The Blob was actually her stepuncle. "We just wanted to make sure things were okay."

"Everything's under control," said The Blob. "There's been some water damage, but it's mainly around the canteen. We'll have a better idea of how bad it is in the morning."

"Can't we go in and see?" Justin asked.

"No," The Blob said curtly. "It's . . . too dangerous. There's water everywhere, and the electricity is on. We don't want anyone to get electrocuted."

"Oh, okay." Justin, Amanda, and I backed away from the door. By now the fire was completely out. A few wisps of smoke rose from some red cinders. We headed back toward the bunkhouse.

"Guess we'll have to see what the dining hall looks like in the morning," Justin said.

"I hope there isn't too much damage," Amanda said.

We kept walking. After a few moments, I realized that both Amanda and Justin were looking at me.

"What is it?" I asked.

"You're being awfully quiet, Lucas," Amanda said. "I can tell you have something on your mind."

"You're right," I admitted. "Remember how The Blob said he didn't want us to go into the dining hall because he was worried we might get electrocuted?"

Amanda and Justin nodded.

"There's just one thing I don't get," I said. "Since when does he care about our safety?"

CHAPTER

11

The next morning Justin and I passed the canteen on our way to the camp kitchen. The canteen door was locked with a big padlock, and a piece of plywood had been nailed up over the counter area. A big handwritten sign said KEEP OUT.

"So, where do astronauts hang out on a computer?" Justin asked.

"I don't know," I said.

"The space bar," Justin said.

I almost smiled.

"I saw that!" Justin cried. "You almost smiled!"

"Almost doesn't count," I said as we went into the kitchen. Even though it was early morning, it was already hot. Bag and the orphan Sherpas were huddled in the industrial-size refrigerator with the door open. Bag was giving them another lesson in English.

"Please be repeating after me," Bag said. "It is being hotter than molasses in January."

"It is being hotter than molasses in January," repeated the orphan Sherpas.

On the other side of the kitchen, Terry was still reading that *Last Place on Earth* book.

"I bet you didn't know that the British and the Norwegians had a race to see who could be the first to reach the South Pole," he said.

Justin nodded. "You're definitely right about that."

"Guess what happened?" Terry asked.

"Uh, someone won the race?" Justin guessed.

"The Norwegians all came back alive, while the British all froze to death," Terry said.

"Bummer," said Justin.

"Talk about bummers," I whispered, nodding at the kitchen door as The Blob stepped through. He was wearing a bright pink polo shirt with major-league sweat stains under the armpits. And lime green pants and brown-and-white golf shoes. He patted the sweat from his broad forehead with a handkerchief.

Terry quickly put down his book. "Uh, what can I do for you this morning, Mr. Kirby?"

Uuurp! The owner of the camp let out a burp. Then he ripped open a packet of ketchup and sucked on it as he scanned the kitchen with his beady little eyes. "What's for breakfast this morning?"

31

"Well, er, that's a bit of a problem," Terry said. "All we have are some boxes of Raisin Bran, Peanut Butter Crunch, and green, red, and white Rice Krispies for Christmas."

"So what's the problem?" The Blob asked.

"Last time I put cold cereal out, the campers nearly had a riot fighting over the ones they liked while the ones they didn't like never got eaten."

"Please be excusing me, Mr. Kirby," Bag interrupted. "I am being unable to think of a phrase to describe how hot it is being."

"Hot enough to melt snot," The Blob replied.

"I am being very thankful to you." Bag returned to the orphan Sherpas in the refrigerator. "Please be repeating after me. It is being hot enough to melt snot. . . ."

The Blob frowned. "What are they doing in the refrigerator?"

"The Sherpas can't take the heat," Terry explained. "The climate inside the refrigerator is like the weather they're used to."

"Tell them to get out," The Blob said. "My electric bill is bad enough without cooling off half a dozen Sherpas. And mix all the cereals together. That way it'll all be the same and there'll be nothing for the campers to fight about."

Terry told Bag and the Sherpas to get out of the refrigerator, and he told Justin and me to mix the cereals together. Then he turned back to The Blob.

"I'm afraid we have another problem. The milk's smelling a little sour."

"Put it in the freezer for a while," The Blob replied. "The colder it gets, the less it'll smell. And add chocolate syrup to it, too. That'll mask the taste."

Terry grimaced at the thought. "The campers are gonna have to mix all those cereals with half-sour chocolate milk?"

The Blob shrugged. "If they're hungry enough, they'll eat anything."

CHAPTER

12

Justin and I had just finished mixing all the cereals into a big aluminum bowl when The Blob came toward us. "You boys know how to use a saw and a hammer?"

Justin and I nodded.

"Come with me," The Blob said.

"Wait a minute!" Terry gasped. "They're my assistant cooks."

"I'm going to need them for a few days," said The Blob.

"Then who's going to cook?" Terry asked.

"Them." The Blob pointed at Bag and the orphan Sherpas.

"Are you serious?" Terry asked. "They don't even speak English."

"This is not being true," Bag corrected him. "They are being able to speak very fine English." He turned to the orphans. "Please be repeating after me. It is hot enough to melt snot. We are needing a tall, cool glass of booger juice."

The orphans repeated it. Bag beamed proudly.

"Sounds good to me," said The Blob.

"This is ridiculous!" Terry sputtered. "I'll never have time to cook enough food to feed everyone."

"Sure you will," said The Blob. "You just won't have time to visit your girlfriend." Then he turned to Justin and me. "You two, come with me."

We followed The Blob out of the kitchen and across the dining hall to the canteen. Amanda was already there, dressed in a white T-shirt and jeans. Around her waist was a carpenter's belt with a hammer hanging from it. "Hey, guys," she said.

"The canteen floor was damaged by all the water from last night," said The Blob. "The floor has to be taken up and a new one laid down. This morning your job will be to pull up the old floor and throw it out."

"Are we going to put a new floor down?" Amanda asked.

"You'll help the carpenter do that," The Blob said. "He'll be here later."

"What are the campers going to do about candy?" Justin asked.

"They'll have to live without it," said The Blob. "All the candy was ruined by the water. I've ordered more, but it'll take time to get here. Now, get to work."

Using pry bars and hammers, Amanda, Justin, and I started to pull up the old floor in the canteen.

"So what kind of dog is full of ticks?" Justin asked.

Amanda and I shared a weary look. It seemed like he just couldn't stop telling jokes.

"A watchdog, Justin," Amanda said, as if the answer was totally obvious.

Justin shook his head in wonder. "You are good, Amanda. But here's one you'll never get. What has four wheels and goes splash?"

"Hmmm." Amanda pressed her finger against her lips and thought about it. "A car pool!"

Justin's jaw dropped. "Unbelievable!"

"Hey, what happened to the canteen?" a voice asked behind us. We turned around and found a couple of campers looking in through the doorway.

"It got flooded," Justin answered.

"Where's the candy?" one of the campers asked.

"Wrecked by the water," said Justin.

The campers looked shocked. "There's no candy?"

"Nope."

"What are we supposed to eat?" they asked.

"Camp food," Justin said.

"Are you mental?" one of them asked. "Do you know what they did this morning? They mixed up Raisin Bran with some peanut butter cereal and red and green Rice Krispies. And we were supposed to eat it with sour chocolate milk!"

Justin and I shared a guilty look. The campers left, and we went back to work. By midmorning we were almost done. Meanwhile, it had gotten really hot in the canteen. Sweat dripped down our faces as we pulled up the last floorboard.

"That's it," I said, wiping the perspiration off my forehead. "Now we have to wait until the carpenter gets here."

"Let's go into the kitchen and get something cold to drink," Justin said.

"You guys go ahead," said Amanda. "I want to go up to the animal hut and check on Fred."

"How's he doing?" I asked.

"Not well," said Amanda. "I was there this morning, and he hardly budged."

Amanda headed for the animal hut, and Justin and I crossed the dining hall toward the kitchen.

"Get the feeling Fred is on his way to the big coconut tree in the sky?" Justin asked.

"Yeah," I said. "It's too bad. I think Amanda really likes that old monkey."

"When Fred finally bites the big banana, I'm gonna be there to comfort Amanda," Justin said. "She's gonna need a shoulder to cry on."

"That's really admirable of you," I said.

"Thanks," said Justin. "And I mean, it's not gonna have anything to do with the fact that I have a crush on her. I'm gonna do it out of the kindness of my heart. It's the kind of thing I'd do for anyone."

I nodded somberly. "Like, if Brad's favorite pet died, you'd let him cry on your shoulder, too?"

Justin made a face. "Well, I wouldn't go *that* far."

We stepped into the kitchen. Brad was in there, talking to Terry.

"Speak of the devil," Justin whispered to me.

"Let me get this straight," Terry was saying. "Mr. Kirby wants a cheeseburger, fries, a chocolate milk shake, *and* shish kebab?"

Brad nodded. "He's really hungry today."

Terry shook his head. "You're so full of it, Brad. Now, get out of here. When Mr. Kirby's food is ready, I'll send one of the orphans over with it."

Brad pointed an angry finger at Terry. "Someday you're going to be sorry."

"Oh, yeah?" Terry's eyebrows rose. "When?"

"When that big fat girlfriend of yours wants some candy and you can't find any for her," Brad said.

Terry's eyes widened with fury. He grabbed a frying pan and hurled it across the kitchen at Brad's head.

Clang! It banged into the wall. But Brad got the message. He ducked out of the kitchen fast.

"You'd better run, Brad!" Terry shouted after him. "The next time you set foot in this kitchen, you're dead meat!"

"Maybe we could feed him to the campers," I said.

"If Roadkill Man doesn't claim him first," Justin added.

Just then a foul, burning odor filled the kitchen. A head full of long, scraggly gray hair popped through the doorway. The hair was held back by a red bandanna going around the forehead. "Did someone mention my name?"

"It's Roadkill Man!" Justin cried.

CHAPTER

14

"**P**eace, brothers." Roadkill Man held up two fingers in the peace sign. Besides his long, scraggly hair, he had a bushy gray beard and wore ragged old clothes filled with tears and stains. Around his neck were a bunch of colorful beads like the hippies from the 1960s used to wear.

Waving his hand in front of his nose, Justin leaned toward me and whispered, "Did someone cut the cheese?"

"No, it's his body odor," I whispered back.

"What did one eye say to the other?" Justin whispered.

"What?" I whispered.

"Just between us, something smells."

Wherever Roadkill Man went, he brought with him a powerful stench of body odor mixed with rotting flesh. Roadkill Man lived off the dead animals that got run over in the road. He usually walked around with a stick and an old burlap bag for carrying squashed animals. But today he was carrying a wrinkled old brown paper bag with grease stains all over it. In his other hand was a long green metal toolbox.

"What are you doing here?" Justin asked, wiping a tear out of his eye. Roadkill Man's BO was so potent it made our eyes water.

"Mr. Kirby called me this morning," Roadkill Man replied. "He said he needed a carpenter."

"I thought you were against all forms of work," I said.

"I am," Roadkill Man said. "But I've got a special occasion coming up and I need to subjugate myself to the lure of the capitalist currency."

Justin and I both looked at Terry. "What's he talking about?"

"He has to make some money," Terry answered.

"I guess you have tools in the toolbox," I said. "But what's in the greasy paper bag?"

"Lunch," Roadkill Man replied. "Chicken."

"Chicken?" Justin frowned. "I thought you only eat roadkill."

"That's correct," Roadkill Man said, holding up the greasy bag. "Behold the chicken that *failed* to cross the road. Now, let's get to work."

Justin and I led him out of the kitchen and through

the dining hall to the canteen. We were just about to go in when I heard a scraping sound inside. I turned to Justin and Roadkill Man and pressed a finger to my lips.

"There's someone in there," I whispered, and pushed open the canteen door. Inside, a surprised-looking camper was on his hands and knees. It was Ralphie, the red-haired barf champ.

"What are you doing?" I asked.

Ralphie slowly rose to his feet. "I . . . I was looking for candy."

"It was all ruined by the water," I said.

"I . . . I thought I'd look, anyway," Ralphie stammered. "Maybe a piece got left behind. I'm starving."

"I hate to say this, Ralphie," Justin said, "but I think you're gonna have to eat the camp food."

Ralphie turned pale and trembled. "You know I always barf it right back up. I've been living on candy since camp began. You guys wouldn't have anything sweet, would you? An M&M or a malted-milk ball? Even a Tic Tac!"

"I've got some chicken." Roadkill Man held up the greasy paper bag. "Scraped off Route 43 less than two hours ago." He reached into the bag and pulled out a drumstick. It looked like normal fried chicken, except for some black spots.

"What are those black spots?" Ralphie asked.

"Road tar," said Roadkill Man. "Helps make the bread crumbs stick. Like to try it?"

"Road tar?" Ralphie clamped his hand over his mouth and raced out of the canteen. A moment later we heard loud barfing sounds from outside.

Roadkill Man scratched his head. "Guess that means no."

"That kid doesn't know what he's missing," Roadkill Man said, taking a big bite out of the drumstick. The canteen door opened again, and Amanda trudged in. Her shoulders were stooped, and her eyes were downcast.

"Bad news?" I asked.

She nodded sadly. "Fred's not going to last much longer."

"Who's Fred?" Roadkill Man asked.

"A rhesus monkey up in the animal hut," Amanda replied.

"A monkey!?" Roadkill Man's eyes widened, and he licked his lips. "Got much flesh on him?"

Amanda frowned. "Why do you ask?"

It was obvious to me why Roadkill Man had asked. Before he could answer, I said, "Uh, forget it. So why don't we get to work on the floor?"

We worked all afternoon and into the night on the

canteen floor. We probably didn't have to work that hard, but after seeing Ralphie so desperate for candy, I figured the sooner we repaired the canteen, the sooner he and his friends could start eating sweets again.

Finally it was late and dark, and we were tired. Amanda said she was going back to the animal hut to check on Fred.

Roadkill Man, Justin, and I started back through the dark toward the bunkhouse.

"Would you really eat that old monkey?" Justin asked Roadkill Man.

"Better believe it," Roadkill Man replied. "Monkey meat is considered a delicacy in Central and South America. I developed a taste for it back when I lived on a commune in Costa Rica. Man, I can't begin to tell you how much I'd love some."

"Especially after eating the same old squashed skunks and greasy gophers for years, right?" I guessed.

"Right," said Roadkill Man.

"So what's that special occasion you were talking about?" Justin asked him.

Before Roadkill Man could answer, a whisper came out of the shadows: "Hey, guys!"

We stopped and looked around.

"Over here," the voice whispered. It was coming from a dark clump of trees. Roadkill Man, Justin, and I went over. In the shadows we could see a camper behind the trees, holding something in his hands. Justin and I couldn't see what it was.

"Check it out." The kid held up a Vega deluxe hand video game. "Brand-new game gear. I'll sell it to you for fifty bucks."

"I don't have fifty bucks," I said.

"Come on, it's new," the camper said. "I'll even throw in some of the games."

"That's really nice of you, but we still can't buy it," Justin said.

"How about forty bucks?" the kid asked. "Could you handle that?"

Justin and I shook our heads.

"Well, I'll be seeing you guys tomorrow." Roadkill Man waved and disappeared into the dark. He had no interest in the game.

"Thirty?" the camper asked, sounding desperate.

"It's a really great offer," I said. "But I don't think my friend and I are interested."

"Twenty-five?" the camper persisted.

"Are you crazy?" Justin said. "That thing is worth way more than twenty-five bucks. Why are you so desperate to sell it?"

"I need money," the camper said.

"For what?" I asked.

The camper looked around as if he wanted to make sure no one was listening. "Candy," he said in a low voice.

"Candy doesn't cost that much," I said.

"And there's none around, anyway," added Justin.

"Wrong and wrong," the kid replied. "It's around, and it costs plenty."

"You mean someone is selling it?" I asked.

"Look," the camper said. "I've already told you more than I should have. Twenty bucks for the game gear is my final offer. Take it or leave it."

Justin and I both shook our heads. The camper muttered something angrily under his breath, then disappeared into the dark.

CHAPTER

16

"**D**o you get the feeling that someone is running a black-market candy operation?" Justin asked as we walked into the bunkhouse.

"Sure sounds like it," I said. "I guess there's always someone who'll try to make money off other people's misery."

Inside the bunkhouse, Terry was lying on his bunk, reading. It was hot. Justin wiped some sweat off his forehead. "That book still keeping you cool?"

"Naw, but it's a good story, anyway," Terry said. "You had these Norwegian dudes racing against these British dudes. Both groups had sled dogs to pull their sleds across the ice and snow."

"That reminds me," Justin said. "Know where they keep sled dogs at night?"

Terry scratched his head. "No."

"In a *mush* room," Justin said.

Terry looked perplexed.

"When you want sled dogs to start pulling, you yell 'mush' at them," I explained.

Terry scowled and looked back at Justin. "That's supposed to be funny?"

Justin shrugged. "Guess not."

Terry pointed at the book. "It took the Norwegians and the British a lot longer to reach the South Pole than they expected. Both groups ran out of food. Guess why the Norwegians came back alive while the British froze to death?"

"The Norwegians wore warmer clothes?" Justin guessed.

"Nope," said Terry. "Each time one of their dogs died, the Norwegians ate it."

Justin and I probably should have been totally grossed out. But after knowing Roadkill Man, eating dead animals was starting to sound normal.

"So guess why the British died?" Terry asked.

"They had smaller dogs?" Justin guessed.

"They refused to eat their dogs," Terry said. "They thought it was undignified. So what does that tell you? I mean, what's the lesson in all this?"

"When in doubt, eat a dog?" I guessed.

Terry sighed and shook his head. "Think about it." Then he stuck his face back in the book.

Justin and I got out of our kitchen clothes, washed up, and climbed into our beds.

"You know, Justin," I said in a low voice, "so far this summer we've met one guy who eats roadkill and another who reads books about people who eat dogs. I may never look at food the same way again."

"That reminds me of a joke," Justin said. "Do you know the difference between a piece of steak and an old shoe?"

"No."

"Good, then you can eat the shoe."

CHAPTER

The next morning we headed for the camp kitchen to rustle up some breakfast before getting back to work on the canteen floor. It was early. The grass was wet with dew, and the sun was still behind the trees to the east. As we got closer to the entrance of the dining hall, we noticed a camper sitting on the front step. That was weird because the campers at Run-a-Muck usually slept late.

When the camper saw us, he jumped up and ran into the dining hall.

"I bet he's a lookout," I said, starting to jog. "Come on, let's see what's going on."

Justin and I ran to the dining hall. As we pushed through the doors, we saw a dozen campers scatter like cockroaches before a light. Justin and I went into the kitchen.

The place looked like it had been hit by a tornado. Cabinets were open, and jars and bins were overturned, spilling flour and salt on the counters.

"Unbelievable!" Justin gasped.

A scraping sound came from behind the stainless-steel counters. I quickly pressed my fingers to my lips and motioned for Justin to follow.

We tiptoed toward the counters. Just as we got there, a camper jumped up and made a run for it. I managed to grab him and twist one of his hands behind his back.

"Let me go! Let me go!" he cried. He had chocolate smears around his mouth.

"What were you doing in here?" I asked.

"We were desperate," the camper gasped. "We couldn't help ourselves."

"Desperate for what?" Justin asked.

"Candy, sugar," the kid said. "Anything sweet. It didn't matter."

"They must've found the chocolate chips," I said, looking at the chocolate smears around his mouth.

"It wasn't just me," the kid cried. "There were a bunch of us. Please don't tell The Blob. Don't turn me in."

"Okay, get lost," I said, letting the kid go.

But the kid didn't run. "You guys work here, right? That means you know where everything is." He quickly undid his wristwatch. "I'll sell you this watch cheap. It was a present from my grandparents and it's really valuable. But it's yours if you tell me where something sweet is."

"Sorry." I shook my head.

"Aw, come on, *please*?" the kid begged.

"I would if I knew," I said. "But it looks like you guys got everything we had."

The kid hung his head and trudged out of the kitchen. Justin and I shared a look.

"This," I said, "is getting really bad."

CHAPTER

But it got even worse. Soon we couldn't go anywhere without campers offering us expensive CD players, tennis rackets, fishing gear, and small, handheld TVs. And they were willing to sell them for almost nothing.

We heard a rumor that you could only get candy from someone called the Candyman. The prices were ridiculous. A jawbreaker cost five dollars. A pack of gum ten dollars. A candy bar fifteen to twenty dollars!

"I don't know who this Candyman is, but he must be making a fortune," Justin said as we worked with Roadkill Man and Amanda to lay the new floor in the canteen.

"He'd better enjoy it while he can," said Amanda. "Because as soon as the canteen is finished and the new candy comes in, the prices are going back to normal. You wouldn't believe what happened this morning when I went to check on Fred. You know that specially sweetened formula I give him? When I got to the animal hut, I found a camper *eating* the stuff."

"Eating *monkey* food?" I said.

"I could barf," Justin groaned.

"So how is the old monkey?" Roadkill Man asked.

"He's really sick," Amanda said sadly. "I'm afraid that it's just a matter of days."

Roadkill Man nodded sympathetically, but I knew what he was thinking. Once Fred bit the big banana, there had to be a way to turn him into Fredburgers.

"By the way," I said to him. "You still haven't told us why you're doing this carpentry work."

Before Roadkill Man could answer, we were interrupted by a sudden and loud fracas coming from out in the dining hall.

"Hey! Gimme that!"

"No, it's mine!"

Crash! Thwack! Crunk!

"What's going on?" Roadkill Man asked.

Amanda looked at her watch. "Mail call."

"Let go!" someone screamed.

Thawmp!

"I got it!"

"Cowabunga!"

"Let's take a look," I said. We left the canteen. In the dining hall kids were fighting and wrestling each other to the ground. A kid got thrown out of the rumble and landed on the floor near us. His hair was disheveled, one of his eyes was swollen, and his lip was bleeding.

"What's going on?" I asked.

"Someone got a care package from home," the kid gasped. "There's a pack of M&M's in it!" The kid dove back into the brawl.

On the stage, a counselor called out, "Ricky Pulger," and held up a big cardboard box.

"Here!" Ricky, the kid we'd found wrapped in toilet paper, fought his way through the crowd to get his package. The counselor started to hand it to him. But a big kid with short brown hair and an earring grabbed the box away.

"Hey!" Ricky cried. "That's mine!"

A bunch of campers tore through Ricky's package. Pieces of cardboard, brand-new underwear, and rolls of extra-soft toilet paper flew in the air. The big kid found a white plastic bottle and tried to run. But the other campers pounced on him and started fighting for it.

"Hey!" Ricky shouted. "Those are *my* vitamins!"

"Vitamins?" Justin frowned.

"They must be the chewable, sweet ones," I said.

"Brad Schmook," the counselor on stage called, holding up a large white cardboard box. We watched Brad fight his way through the crowd to the stage to get the box. Instantly, a pack of crazed-looking campers surrounded him.

"Forget it," Brad told them. "This isn't candy."

"Why should we believe you?" one of the campers demanded.

"Look." Brad tore open the box and showed them what was inside. "It's a mini-CD tape sound system. Now I can listen to *The Best of Sinatra*."

The pack of starving campers turned away. Brad started out of the dining hall with his new sound system.

"Too bad," Justin said. "It would have been cool to see them tear Brad's box apart."

"Those mini-CD systems are pretty expensive, aren't they?" I asked.

Justin nodded. "They cost a ton of money. Why?"

"I was just wondering," I said. "Where would Brad get that kind of money?"

CHAPTER

19

We worked all day on the floor of the canteen. By nightfall, we were almost done.

"Well, that's pretty much it," Roadkill Man said, dusting off his hands. "We'll sand and paint in the morning, and the job will be finished."

"I guess you can reopen the canteen tomorrow afternoon," Justin said to Amanda.

"Let's go tell The Blob we're finished," I said.

"I'll go with you," said Roadkill Man. "Maybe I can get him to hand over my pay."

We started toward The Blob's house. As we passed the rec hall, a thin band of red light appeared in the air above us. For a second I thought it was a UFO, but then it settled onto the grass at our feet. The lights dimmed and I picked it up.

"Cool," said Justin. "A Frisbee with lights."

Ralphie, the camp barf champion, stepped out of the dark. "Can I have it back?"

I gave it back to him. "I've never seen a Frisbee with lights before. Where'd it come from?"

"I made it," Ralphie said.

"How?" I asked.

"A couple of small lights, a microchip, and a little battery," Ralphie said. "Centrifugal force makes it go on."

Ralphie walked off into the dark and we continued toward The Blob's house.

"We've been working really long hours," Justin said as we walked. "Maybe The Blob'll give us a day off as a reward."

"Don't hold your breath," Amanda said.

"You never told us what you needed the money for," I said to Roadkill Man as we walked.

"Big secret," Roadkill Man said. "I hope Mr. Kirby has some other jobs, because I need more."

The Blob lived in a big yellow and white house on the side of the hill behind the camp. It was surrounded by colorful gardens of flowers. Beside the house was The Blob's private eighteen-hole golf course. No one from Camp Run-a-Muck, except Brad the Cad, was allowed to go near it.

Grrrrrrrrrrr . . . As we got close to The Blob's house, The Blob Dog started to growl. The Blob Dog was a big, squat, black-and-white bulldog. Big globs of saliva dripped from the corners of his mouth. He looked a lot like The Blob.

Groof! Groof! The Blob Dog started barking.

Justin hesitated. "Maybe this isn't such a good idea."

"Don't worry," I said. "The Blob Dog is in his pen."

"It's not the dog I'm worried about," Justin said. "It's The Blob."

"He's my stepuncle," Amanda said. "I'm not proud of it. But it also means that he probably won't be mean to us."

Justin sighed nervously. "If you say so."

We went up to the front door and rang the bell.

"Who is it?" The Blob bellowed from inside.

"It's me, Uncle Bob," Amanda called.

A moment later the front door swung open. The Blob was wearing a white T-shirt and the biggest pair of boxer shorts I'd ever seen. He had a slice of pizza in one hand and red tomato sauce stains around his mouth.

"What can I do for you, Amanda?" he asked.

"We just want you to know that we'll be finished with the canteen tomorrow," Amanda said.

The Blob blinked his beady eyes. He looked as if he'd totally forgotten there was anything wrong with the canteen in the first place. "Oh, uh, that's good news."

"So we can reopen tomorrow afternoon," Amanda said.

"And I was wondering if I could get paid," said Roadkill Man.

The Blob's wide forehead creased into thick, fat furrows. "You haven't finished the job."

"All we have to do is paint," said Roadkill Man.

"You'll get paid when the job's done," said The Blob. "Not before then."

"What about the new candy?" Amanda asked.

The Blob gave her a blank look.

"You have it, don't you?" Amanda asked.

"Uh . . . no," The Blob said. "It hasn't come yet."

"Then it must be coming soon, right?" Amanda asked.

"Uh . . . sure," The Blob answered. "Sure, it's coming soon."

"Because the kids are dying for it," Amanda said.

"Right," said The Blob.

"So you'll let me know as soon as the candy gets here, won't you, Uncle Bob?" Amanda asked.

"Yes, absolutely," The Blob said.

An awkward moment passed.

"Is there anything else?" The Blob asked.

"Well, uh, there is one thing," Justin said nervously. "We've been working sixteen-hour days to fix the canteen floor. Now that we're almost finished, we were wondering if we could get a day off."

"No." The Blob turned and slammed the door closed.

We started back toward the bunkhouse.

"I guess I shouldn't be surprised," Justin moped as

we walked back through the dark. "The Blob'll never give us an extra day off."

"I just hope he pays me," Roadkill Man said, nervously chewing on a dirty fingernail. "I really need the money."

"I hope the candy comes soon, or the campers are going to go berserk," said Amanda.

Somewhere in the distance a cow mooed.

"Hey, what's a cow's favorite party game?" Justin asked.

"Not now, Justin," I groaned.

"Hold on," Amanda said. "I'll think of it . . . uh, moosical chairs?"

"You are incredible!" Justin said.

We reached the bunkhouse and said good-bye to Roadkill Man.

"You think Mr. Kirby will pay me for my work, don't you?" he asked Amanda.

"I think so," Amanda said. "I mean, I know my stepuncle's pretty sleazy, but I don't think he's totally dishonest."

Roadkill Man nodded. "Okay, see you tomorrow."

We watched him walk off into the woods.

"For a guy who says he doesn't care about money, he sure seems to care a lot about it now," Justin said.

"Yeah," I had to agree. "It makes you wonder."

"Know what else makes me wonder?" Amanda asked. "Why it's so quiet tonight."

She was right. Usually after dinner, campers were

outside playing ball, having water fights, and generally goofing around and having fun. But tonight the camp was oddly still. A few campers were out, but they were just sitting around talking or staring off into space.

"It's like no one has the energy to do anything," Justin said.

"You're right," I said. "It's because they don't have any candy. What a bummer! Kids at camp are supposed to have fun, but they need energy. And around here they get their energy from candy. This candy problem is really getting bad."

CHAPTER

20

Amanda went into the girls' staff cabin, and we went into the bunkhouse. Inside, it was dark and empty.

"Where is everyone?" Justin asked, looking around.

"Don't have a clue," I said.

"*Uhhhhhnnnnn...*" A moaning sound came from the bathroom.

"Now what?" I asked. We went into the bathroom and turned on the light. It looked empty.

"*Uhhhhhnnnnn...*" There was that groaning sound again.

"It's from the showers," Justin said.

We went into the shower room. The curtain to one of the shower stalls was closed. Justin pulled it open and gasped.

Little Ricky Pulger was sprawled on the floor of the shower. His eyes were glassy. An empty tube of toothpaste was clutched tightly in his hand. A beard of white foam dripped from his mouth and hung from his chin.

"He got the toothpaste," I said.

"This has gotten way out of control," said Justin.

"Come on," I said, reaching for one of Ricky's arms. "Let's get you cleaned up."

We helped Ricky to his feet. Justin turned on the cold water, and we doused him.

Ricky blinked as he came out of his stupor. "Wha . . . ? What happened?"

"You got into the toothpaste," I said.

"Oh, man," Ricky groaned. "I couldn't help it. I'm really sorry — "

"We know," Justin said. "You were desperate for something sweet."

Ricky nodded. His face was red with embarrassment. We helped him out of the shower and through the bunkhouse.

"Think you'll be okay?" I asked as we stepped outside.

"For now," Ricky said, standing there in his dripping wet camp clothes. "But I know what's gonna happen. Sooner or later I'm gonna need something sweet. I'm gonna have to have it. I'm gonna do anything for it."

"We understand," Justin said grimly.

Ricky headed off into the dark toward his cabin. Justin and I were just about to go back inside when Justin pointed to the girls' staff cabin.

Amanda was sitting on the steps. Her chin was propped in her hands, and she looked really bummed. We went over. Amanda gave us a crooked smile.

"What's wrong?" I asked.

"On my last day off I bought a small jug of real maple syrup," she said. "I was going to send it to my little sister. But I just looked in my cubby and it's gone."

Without saying a word, we all knew what had happened and why.

"We have to do something about this," I said. "We can't just stand by and watch these kids be so miserable."

Crick! A twig snapped in the dark. Not far from us two campers were sneaking through the woods. Then one of them mumbled something about "Candyman."

I turned back to Justin and Amanda. "Come on, let's see where they're going."

CHAPTER

21

We let the two campers go ahead into the dark woods, then quietly followed them.

"Think they're going to the pizza place?" Justin whispered as we made our way through the trees and underbrush. Log Cabin Pizza was a mile or two down the road.

"I don't remember it having any candy," I said. "Do you?"

Amanda and Justin shook their heads. Ahead of us the two campers took a turn and headed up a hill.

"Hey!" Justin gasped. "Isn't this the hill where Roadkill Man's cave is?"

"You're right," I whispered back.

"You think Roadkill Man's also the Candyman who's ripping kids off?" Amanda asked.

"He did say he really needed money," Justin said.

It seemed hard to believe. Then again, just about

everything that happened at Camp Run-a-Muck seemed hard to believe.

The two kids continued uphill through the trees. The moon was out, and as we climbed higher it seemed to get brighter. Up ahead we could see the big, flat, round rock that served as the front door to Roadkill Man's cave.

But the kids climbed right past it!

"Now what?" Amanda whispered as we followed.

"Where are they going?" Justin wondered out loud. "There's nothing else up here."

"The forest rangers' tower," I said. At the very top of the hill was an old wooden tower. At the top of the tower was a shack where forest rangers used to watch for fires.

"But that's crazy," Justin said. "Why would anyone go there for candy?"

"Shhh!" I pressed a finger to my lips. "Let's get closer. Maybe we'll find out."

The two campers reached the top of the hill and crossed the clearing to the base of the tower. Justin, Amanda, and I hid behind some bushes at the edge of the clearing and watched as one of the campers cupped his hands around his mouth and called up. "Hey, Candyman!"

At the top of the tower, a dark figure stepped out into the moonlight. "What do you want?" he called down.

"Two boxes of M&M's, one Good & Plenty, three packs of Bubblicious, and five jawbreakers," the camper replied.

"A hundred bucks." The Candyman lowered something by a rope.

"What is it?" Amanda whispered.

"A basket," I whispered back.

When the basket got down to the campers, they put the money in it. Then the Candyman pulled the basket back up.

"So they don't know who the Candyman is, either," Amanda whispered.

"Gee, whoever figured this scheme out was pretty smart," Justin said.

In the moonlight we watched the Candyman take the money out of the basket and count it. Then he put some things in the basket and sent it down again.

"Here comes the candy," Justin whispered.

The basket reached the campers. They grabbed the candy and headed toward us.

"Duck!" I hissed.

We ducked down behind the bushes so the campers wouldn't see us. They seemed so eager to get back to the camp that I doubt they would have noticed us, anyway. A moment later they disappeared down the hill and into the dark.

"Now what?" Justin asked.

"I think we should pay the Candyman a visit,"

Amanda said. "I think we should find out who he is and let him know we don't like the way he's ripping off the campers."

"Wait," I said.

"Why?" asked Justin.

"I think I hear something," I whispered. "Listen."

In the moonlight, the faint strains of music drifted down to us from the forest ranger tower.

"What's that?" Justin whispered.

"It sounds like something my grandparents used to listen to," whispered Amanda.

Suddenly I realized what it was. My grandparents had also listened to it.

"That," I said, "is *The Best of Sinatra.*"

"**T**hen the Candyman is Brad!" Justin gasped.

"Shhh!" I pressed my finger to my lips. "You want him to hear us?"

"I don't believe it," Justin whispered angrily. "In fact, I think we should go up there and give him a knuckle sandwich to chew on. I'd like him to see how *that* tastes."

"I should have known it was Brad," Amanda grumbled. "Who else would be so low and greedy?"

"Come on, Lucas," Justin urged me. "Let's go teach him a lesson."

"Wait," I whispered. "Remember what you said before? That whoever set up this scam was really smart?"

"So?" Justin said.

"You really think Brad the Cad had the brains to think of this all by himself?" I asked.

"You're right," Amanda said. "There must be someone else involved."

CHAPTER

23

It wasn't long before Brad climbed down out of the tower. He was wearing a small backpack. We followed him back to camp. I can't say I was really surprised to see him go past the bunkhouse and rec hall. I had a feeling he had to go somewhere else first.

"Listen, guys, I think I'm going to bag it," Amanda said with a yawn. "If you find out anything new, tell me in the morning, okay?"

"Sure thing," I said.

Amanda headed for the girls' staff cabin. Justin and I stayed on Brad's trail — straight to The Blob's house!

"Why aren't I surprised?" I groaned as we hid behind a tree and watched Brad knock on The Blob's door.

The door opened, and there stood The Blob.

"You won't believe how much we made tonight!" Brad blurted.

"Shut up and come in," The Blob grumbled, looking around warily. "You want the whole world to hear you?"

Brad stepped into the house. *Bang!* The door slammed behind him.

"You were right," Justin said, backing away. "I should have known Brad wasn't smart enough to think of this scam on his own."

"Where are you going?" I asked.

"To bed," Justin said. "What's the point of hanging around?"

"We can sneak closer," I said. "Maybe we'll overhear them."

Justin bit his lip nervously. "What about The Blob Dog?"

"He should be in his pen," I said.

Justin sighed reluctantly and followed as I snuck closer to the house.

"Hey, Lucas," he whispered. "What should you do if you see a killer dog?"

"I don't know," I whispered back.

"Pray he doesn't see you," Justin said.

We crept around to the back of the house. A light was on in the kitchen. Inside we could hear The Blob and Brad talking.

"Here's your share of the money," The Blob said. "You're right. This was the best night yet."

"At this rate we'll be rich by the end of the summer," Brad said.

"Maybe, but we have a problem," The Blob replied. "Amanda and her two friends fixed the canteen floor much faster than I expected. Amanda wants to start selling the new supply of candy right away."

"But there is no new supply of candy," Brad said.

"Of course there isn't, you idiot," The Blob grumbled. "I never bothered to order it. With all the candy left from the canteen there was no point. The problem is, Amanda and her friends don't know that. They think all the old candy was destroyed in the flood."

"Okay, okay," Brad said. "Tomorrow night I'll start another fire near the dining hall. Then I'll go inside and set off the water sprinklers again. We'll have another flood in the canteen."

"You don't think having another flood will look just *a little* suspicious?" The Blob scoffed.

"Uh, I guess you're right," Brad allowed.

"For now we'll just keep doing what we've been doing," said The Blob. "If Amanda asks why the new supply of candy hasn't arrived, I'll tell her the shipment was delayed. In the meantime, you've got the candy safe and hidden?"

"I sure do," Brad said.

"And there's plenty left?" The Blob asked.

"You bet," said Brad. "At fifteen and twenty bucks a candy bar, we'll practically be millionaires by the end of the summer."

Grrrrrrrrrrr . . . Before we could hear The Blob's

reply, a deep, throaty growl split the silence. I felt a sudden chill run up my arms and down my spine.

Justin turned pale. "What was that?"

"What do you *think* it was?" I whispered back.

"But I thought you said The Blob Dog was supposed to be locked in his pen," Justin gasped.

I turned slowly. Two evil eyes glared at us through the dark. The moonlight glistened off the pointy white fangs and the globs of saliva hanging below them.

"Don't look now," I groaned. "But he's not in his pen."

Grrrrrrr ... The Blob Dog took a step closer. Justin shut his eyes and pressed his hands together. He turned his face upward, and his lips started to move silently.

"What are you doing?" I whispered.

"I'm praying he doesn't see us," Justin replied.

Grrrrrrr ... The Blob Dog growled.

"I have a feeling it's too late for that," I whispered.

Justin opened his eyes. "Don't move," he whispered. "I read somewhere that they have really bad eyesight. If you don't move, they can't see you."

"That's not *dogs*," I hissed. "It's *bears*."

"Maybe The Blob Dog's got some bear in him," Justin said hopefully.

Grrrrrr ... The Blob Dog stepped closer.

Screeeeekk ... From inside the kitchen came the sound of chair legs scraping as someone stood up.

"You hear the dog growl?" The Blob said. "Someone's out there."

Meanwhile, outside in the dark, I turned to Justin and whispered, "There's only one good thing about bulldogs."

"What's that?" Justin whispered back.

"Their legs are short," I said. "*Run!*"

CHAPTER

25

We ran.

Grrooooof! The Blob Dog barked and ran after us.

"This reminds me of a joke," Justin panted as we sprinted through the dark.

"How can being chased by a killer dog remind you of a joke?" I gasped.

Grrooooof! The Blob Dog barked again.

"Everything reminds me of jokes," Justin said. "So how is a person being chased by a dog like a leaky faucet?"

"I don't know," I said, breathing hard.

"They both run," said Justin.

By the time we got back to the bunkhouse, we'd managed to lose The Blob Dog. I was surprised to find Amanda waiting for us on the front steps.

"What happened?" she asked.

"We ran into The Blob Dog," Justin said, panting hard.

"I thought you were going to sleep," I said to her.

"I tried, but I couldn't sleep," she said. "I was worried."

"No kidding?" Justin said. "You were worried about us? Well, you wouldn't believe what happened. There we were, minding our own business, when your stepuncle's dog attacked! Lucas started to run, but I stayed and fought the beast off! You should have seen us wrestling around on the ground. It was incredible! What a fight!"

Amanda had a slight smile on her face. "What's *really* incredible is that you didn't get a single grass or dirt stain on your clothes."

Justin looked down at himself. An embarrassed grin appeared on his lips. "Oops!"

"To tell you the truth, it's Fred I'm worried about," Amanda said.

"The old monkey?" Justin looked disappointed.

"You won't believe the story with the candy," I said, then told her — how Brad had set the fire near the dining hall and then made the sprinkler system in the canteen go off. How they must have taken out all the candy first. How they had no intention of ordering new candy. Instead, they were now selling the old candy at those incredibly high prices.

"By the end of the summer they'll be rich," Justin said.

"And in the meantime," I added, "this camp is going from a fun place where campers can do anything they want, to Bummer Land."

"I guess that explains how Brad could afford that mini-CD system," Amanda said.

"I'm sorry I had to tell you that your stepuncle is involved," I said.

"It's okay," Amanda said with a shrug. "I had a feeling he might be. Like you said, it was hard to believe that Brad could have thought of a scam like that all by himself. I guess the only question now is what we do about it."

"Funny that you should mention that," I said with a smile.

The next morning Justin and I left the bunkhouse and headed for the dining hall. We planned to meet Amanda there and help Roadkill Man put the finishing touches on the canteen. As we walked across the dew-covered lawn, a camper staggered toward us. He had a dazed look in his eyes. White foam bubbled out of his mouth and dripped off his chin. He clenched a crushed toothpaste tube in his hand.

"Spare any toothpaste?" he asked us.

"Sorry." Justin and I shook out heads.

"Just a squeeze, guys," the kid begged. "Just an *inch!*"

Justin and I kept walking.

"That reminds me of a joke," Justin said. "What kind of tuba is impossible to play?"

"I don't know," I said.

"A tuba toothpaste," he said. "And by the way, you haven't told me the plan."

"I haven't figured it all out yet," I said. "I only know it has to be in two parts. First, we have to find out where the candy is hidden. Remember last night The Blob asked Brad if he had it in a safe place?"

"Yeah," Justin nodded. "And what's the second part?"

"Revenge," I said. "Brad has to pay for causing all this misery and getting rich off it."

"Brad the Cad," Justin muttered. "Schmook the Crook."

We went through the entrance to the dining hall and into the canteen. That powerful Roadkill Man odor started to burn our nostrils, and we knew he was already there. When he saw us, he held up his fingers in a V.

"Peace, brothers," he said.

"Peace, Roadkill Man," I said, wiping a tear from my eye.

"How come you always cry when you see me?" he asked.

I couldn't tell him it was his mega BO so I just said they were tears of joy.

Roadkill Man smiled and handed us some sandpaper. "Start sanding."

Justin and I got down on the floor and began to work.

"Hey, Roadkill Man," Justin said as we sanded the floor. "Have you seen Amanda?"

Before Roadkill Man could answer, the canteen

door swung open. Amanda stood there. Her eyes were red and glistening with tears.

"Wow," said Roadkill Man. "Don't tell me you're glad to see me, too?"

Amanda shook her head and sobbed. "It's Fred! He's dead!"

Justin took off his T-shirt and gave it to Amanda to blow her nose in. We all tried to comfort her.

"Don't forget," Justin said. "Fred was old. He probably led a long and happy monkey life before he kicked the bucket."

"Sure," Roadkill Man agreed. "I bet he did a lot of monkeying around."

"He might have gone ape for all we know," I added.

"Thanks, guys, I really appreciate the kind words." Amanda dabbed the tears from her eyes. "I know it's dumb to get this upset, but Fred was a good monkey. I really liked him."

"So, uh, what do you plan to do with the body?" Roadkill Man asked.

I knew the old hippie was thinking about pan-seared primate. Or maybe spaghetti with monkey meatballs. Or chimp chili.

"I'm glad you asked me that, Roadkill Man," Amanda said with a sniff. "I'd really like to give Fred a proper burial. Since you're a carpenter, I was hoping you would build him a little coffin."

Roadkill Man's leathery forehead wrinkled with disappointment. But then he brightened, and a smile appeared on his lips. "If that's what you want, I'll be glad to do it. I'll start on that coffin just as soon as I finish painting the canteen floor."

"Thanks, Roadkill Man," Amanda said. "I knew I could count on you." Then she turned to us. "I hope you'll understand if I don't help this morning. I want to take a walk and be by myself."

"We understand," I said.

"I could come with you if you wanted," Justin said hopefully.

Amanda gave him a bittersweet smile. She turned and glanced at me for a second, almost as if she wanted me to go with her. But we both knew that would really hurt Justin's feelings.

"Thanks for the offer, Justin," she said. "But I think it would be better if I went alone."

She left, and we got back to work. Roadkill Man seemed awfully cheerful and even whistled as he sanded the floor.

"Hey, Roadkill Man, what are you so happy about?" Justin asked.

"Oh, nothing, nothing at all," Roadkill Man replied.

It wasn't long before we finished sanding the floor.

"Okay, boys, you can go back to the kitchen," Roadkill Man said. "I'll paint the floor, and the job will be finished."

As we left the canteen, Roadkill Man was humming happily to himself.

"I don't get it," Justin said as we walked to the kitchen. "What's with that guy?"

"Well, I can't say for sure, but I think it has something to do with Fred," I said.

"It can't be that," Justin said. "You heard Amanda. She wants Fred to have a proper burial. In a coffin."

I nodded. "And who's going to build the coffin?"

"Roadkill Man," Justin answered.

"And who's probably going to nail the coffin shut after they put Fred in it?" I asked.

"Roadkill Man," Justin replied again.

"So who's the only person who's really going to know whether Fred is in that coffin or not?" I asked.

Justin stopped and stared at me, aghast. "Are you serious? You really think Roadkill Man would put something else in the coffin and then eat Fred the monkey?"

Back in the kitchen, Bag and the orphan Sherpas were hard at work. Terry was still reading *The Last Place on Earth*.

"Welcome back to the kitchen, Lucas and Justin," Bag said when he saw us. "We are being lonely without you."

"Thanks, Bag," Justin said. "I wish I could say that I'm glad to be back."

"You are being understood," said Bag. "But the orphans are being glad you are here, too. They are not being happy standing around the hot stoves all day. They are being happier setting tables and washing dishes."

"Man, I just can't get over this!" Terry exclaimed. "The British guys didn't eat their dogs. They starved and froze to death. The Norwegian guys ate their dogs. And you know what?"

The rest of us shook our heads.

"They actually weighed *more* at the end of the trip than at the beginning!" Terry said.

"That is being quite interesting," Bag said. "But please be excusing me for asking what we are serving to the campers for dinner tonight?"

"Maybe we can find some stray dogs," Justin said. "Or how about The Blob Dog?"

"The Blob Dog is being only one dog," said Bag. "This is not being enough to serve the whole camp."

"There's nothing but leftovers," Terry said. "We'll have to mix everything together and add tomato sauce and cheese."

"Ah, yes." Bag nodded. "This is being called American chop suey, is it not?"

"We can't give the campers that," Justin said. "It's the worst dinner we make. No one ever eats it. And those guys are *starving*."

"But there's no money for food," Terry said.

"Too bad there is being no candy in the canteen," Bag said.

"Unless we can find the candy Brad's hiding," I said.

"Forget it," said Justin. "As long as he keeps that candy hidden, he's gonna get rich. He'll never tell us."

Just then the door to the kitchen swung open, and Brad came in.

"Well, well, look who's here," Justin whispered.

"Special order from Mr. Kirby," Brad announced.

"He wants a sliced steak and cheese hero with onion rings, potato salad, and a chocolate milk shake. And his golfing partner wants shish kebab and a Coke."

Terry looked up from his book. "What golfing partner?"

"Uh, Mr. Smith," Brad said. "Mr. Kirby is playing golf with Mr. Smith today."

"Schmook, you are completely full of it," Terry said.

"It's true!" Brad insisted.

"Oh, yeah?" Terry said. "Well, if Mr. Smith wants shish kebab he can come here himself and ask for it."

Brad stared daggers at Terry, then turned and stomped toward the kitchen door.

"I don't see what you're so ticked about," Justin said to him. "Think of the campers. They'll probably wind up gnawing the bark off trees. At least you can have candy for dinner."

Brad glared back at Justin. "I don't know what you're talking about. There's no candy anywhere." Then he slammed out of the kitchen.

"What a liar," Justin grumbled. "I wish there was a way we could get him to lead us to that candy."

At that moment I happened to look outside. Amanda was coming back from her walk. Suddenly I had an idea. "Know what, Justin? Maybe we can."

CHAPTER

29

I asked Terry if we could take a break. Justin and I went outside and sat down with Amanda under a tree.

"You want me to eat dinner with Brad?" she gasped after I outlined the plan. "No way! I can't stand to even *look* at that creep."

"You'll be doing it for the whole camp," Justin explained. "It's the only way we'll ever get Brad to reveal where the candy's hidden."

"This is a great camp," I said. "But it's a drag if the kids aren't having fun. And they can't have fun without candy."

Amanda nodded. She knew that was true. "What makes you think he'll tell me?"

"Because he's crazy about you," I said. "Just have a nice cozy dinner with him. At the end of dinner tell him how much you'd love a piece of candy for dessert. I promise you he'll get it for you."

"And we'll follow him," Justin added with a grin.

"It sounds like a good plan," Amanda admitted. "There's just one problem. I hear we're having American chop suey tonight. You can't really expect us to eat *that*, can you?"

"It won't be American chop suey," I said. "It'll be Brad's favorite dish. Shish kebab."

Justin gave me a startled look and started to say something. But I shook my head and motioned for him to stay quiet.

CHAPTER

30

Brad was due to come back for The Blob's sliced steak and cheese sandwich any minute. Amanda and I sat down at one of the tables in the dining hall and waited. She swept her blond hair out of her face and smiled, her blue eyes sparkling.

"It's funny to be sitting here with you," she said. "Without Justin around."

I nodded. "I guess he and I are always together, huh?"

Amanda nodded slowly. "I always wonder if you have a girlfriend at home."

"No." I shook my head. "You have a boyfriend?"

"Nope."

For a second, neither of us seemed to know what to say.

"Remember," I finally whispered, "as soon as he comes into the dining hall, start talking to me in a low voice. Just make sure you mention shish kebab loud enough for him to hear."

"Gotcha." Amanda nodded.

The dining hall doors opened, and Brad came in. Amanda started to whisper to me. As Brad passed us, she said "shish kebab" just loud enough for him to hear.

Out of the corner of my eye I saw Brad skid to a halt. He seemed to have a hard time deciding what to do, but finally he started toward our table.

"Uh, excuse me," he said to Amanda, "but did I hear you say something about shish kebab?"

Amanda bit her lip and pretended to be surprised that he'd heard her. "Well, yes."

"What about it?" Brad asked.

"I just got this fantastic recipe from my mom," Amanda said. "I'm dying to try it out tonight. I just hate eating alone."

"Well, I'd really like to try it," I said. "But I have to work in the kitchen. There's no way Terry's going to give me the time off."

"What about Justin?" Amanda asked.

I shook my head. "Forget it. We've been working on that canteen for days. Terry really needs us to help with the American chop suey tonight."

Amanda sighed and pretended to look really disappointed. Meanwhile I could see that Brad was totally dying for her to ask him.

Finally she looked up at him. "Brad, will *you* try my shish kebab?"

"Oh, yeah." Brad's smile couldn't have been any bigger. "You bet I will."

CHAPTER

31

"**Y**ou blew it, Lucas," Justin said when I returned to the kitchen. "There's no way your plan can work."

"Why not?" I asked.

"Because there's no meat for the shish kebab," Justin said.

"That's what you think," I said, then turned to Terry. "Hey, Terry. I bet it's been a real drag these past few nights without Justin and me here to help you cook."

"Better believe it," Terry replied.

"I bet you could use some time off to go visit Doris," I said. "Justin and I can handle the American chop suey."

"In other words, you're up to something and you need to get rid of me," Terry said with a smirk. "Well, it's funny you should suggest it, Lucas. Because I was just thinking the same thing. I think I *will* go see Doris. But I'm warning you: I don't know what you're planning, but if it means any trouble for me, I'll make sure you spend the rest of this summer licking bathrooms clean, understand?"

I nodded. Terry stood up. "Okay, I'm out of here."

"Wait," I said. "What if The Blob wants something special to eat?"

"Oh, right." Terry reached into his pocket and pulled out a key. He tossed it to me. "Here you go, man."

It was the key to The Blob's private refrigerator. The only one in the kitchen with decent food in it.

"Thanks, Terry," I said. "Have fun tonight!"

Terry waved and left the kitchen.

As soon as he was gone, Justin turned to me with wide eyes. "Amazing!" he gasped.

"Piece of cake," I said, tossing the key in the air and catching it. "Or should I say, piece of shish kebab?"

Amanda showed up in the kitchen just before dinnertime. The plan was for her to cook the shish kebab while the campers ate in the dining hall. When the campers were finished, the orphan Sherpas would clean up and set a special table with a tablecloth and candles.

"Ready?" I asked Amanda.

"Just let me find a recipe," she said, going over to the shelf where the cookbooks were. She read through a couple of them before picking a recipe she liked. "Okay, guys, here's what I need," she said. "Potatoes."

"Got 'em," I said.

"Tomatoes."

"I know where they are," said Justin.

"Onions."

"I am being able to find them," said Bag.

"Vinegar."

"This is being as easy as booger juice," said one of the orphan Sherpas.

"This is great," Amanda said as we placed all the ingredients on the counter before her. "There's just one last thing we need. Fresh meat for the kebabs."

I took out the key to The Blob's private refrigerator. "Coming right up."

I went over to the refrigerator and tried to stick the key in the lock.

It wouldn't fit!

I must have had it upside down, so I tried it the other way.

It still wouldn't fit!

"What's the problem?" Justin asked.

"It's this key," I said. "It won't go into the lock."

"Here, let me try," Justin said.

I handed him the key, but he couldn't get it to work, either.

"I hate to say this," Justin said, handing the key back to me. "Terry may have given you a key, but it's not the key to The Blob's private refrigerator."

"But it *has* to be," I said, and tried the lock again. It still wouldn't work.

"We don't have much time," Amanda said. "I really have to start cooking."

Justin and I stared at each other in a panic.

"Is there any other meat, anywhere?" I asked.

Justin shook his head. I looked at Bag.

"The Blob Dog is being meat," Bag suggested.

Justin and I looked at each other again.

"Forget it," Amanda said. "You're not killing a living animal. *Especially* a dog."

"But it's The *Blob* Dog," Justin said.

"I don't care," said Amanda.

"What are we going to do?" Justin asked.

"I am being able to send the orphans out to look for Terry," suggested Bag.

"Thanks, Bag," I said. "But I'm sure he's over at Doris's camp by now. We need some meat to cook *right now*."

Just then the kitchen door swung open, and Roadkill Man came in. He was carrying a small wooden box shaped like a coffin.

"Here it is," he said. "The old monkey's final resting place."

Justin and I stared at each other. Our eyes grew wide. At the exact same time we both cried, "Fred!"

CHAPTER

33

"No!" Amanda said. "Never! It's out of the question!"

The question was whether or not we could turn Fred into monkey kebab for Brad.

"But think of the service you'll be doing to the campers," Justin said.

"I don't care," Amanda insisted stubbornly. "You are *not* turning my monkey into Brad Schmook's dinner."

Time was running out. Brad would be coming for dinner in just a few moments. Suddenly I had an idea. Terry had left that book *The Last Place on Earth* in the kitchen. I held it up for Amanda to see.

I told her what the book was about. How the Norwegians had managed to survive their trip to the South Pole by eating their dogs. And how the British had refused to eat their dogs and had died as a result.

"But we're not going to the South Pole," Amanda said.

"That's not the point," I said. "The point is that these dogs were heroes. They served an important cause. The Norwegians toasted each dog before they ate him."

"I don't care if you toast him, bake him, or fry him," Amanda said. "I won't allow it."

"No! No!" I gasped. "They didn't *toast* the dogs like in a toaster. They toasted them with a drink. It was an honor. Those dogs became some of the most famous canines of all time. They went down in *history*. People will always know that if it weren't for those dogs, the Norwegians would have died, and the South Pole might not have been discovered for another fifty years."

"And not only that," Justin added. "You've seen the campers around here. They're starving to death. Think of the service you'll be doing them."

Amanda didn't reply. She actually seemed to be wavering.

"Am I being allowed to join this conversation?" Bag asked.

"Sure, Bag," Amanda said. "Tell us what you think."

"I am thinking that this poor monkey Fred is already being very dead," said Bag. "Therefore it is probably not making a great deal of difference whether he is being eaten by Brad or the little bugs and worms that live in the ground."

Good point! I thought, giving Bag the thumbs-up sign.

CHAPTER

34

Amanda sighed and shook her head sadly. "I'm sorry, but I can't let you cook Fred. Even if it means the campers will have to pay those horrible prices for candy and make Brad and my uncle rich. And please stop trying to make me change my mind."

We nodded silently. It couldn't have been easy for Amanda to make that decision. We had to respect it.

I looked around the room. "Is there anyone here who knows where we can get *any* kind of meat for the shish kebab?"

No one said a thing. It looked like our plan was ruined. Without shish kebab, Amanda would never be able to get Brad the Cad to reveal where the candy was hidden. . . .

The kitchen door opened. A large woman stepped in. She wore a red bandanna around her head, and her long, greasy gray hair was braided into pigtails. Half a dozen strings of colorful beads hung from her neck, and she wore a loose, tentlike yellow-and-red paisley dress. Over one shoulder she carried a burlap bag. In her other hand was a walking stick. A strong odor emanated from her. Justin pinched his nose closed.

"Honey!" Roadkill Man cried.

"Babycakes!" the big woman screeched, and dropped her bag and stick.

They ran to each other and fell into a passionate embrace in the middle of the kitchen. The skinny Roadkill Man almost disappeared in her fleshy arms.

"I've missed you so much!" the woman cried.

"And I've missed you!" Roadkill Man replied.

The rest of us watched in amazement. The stench from the two of them was almost overwhelming.

"What's going on?" Amanda asked.

"Well, I can't say for certain," I said. "But I have a feeling we've just met *Mrs*. Roadkill Man."

CHAPTER

35

When the hugging and kissing finally ended, Roadkill Man turned to the rest of us. "I'd like you all to meet my wife, Mrs. Roadkill Man. This is the big occasion I've been telling you about. For the last month she's been on an extended walking tour, looking for new forms of roadkill to eat."

"And you'll never guess what I found for you behind a pet store in Springfield," Mrs. Roadkill Man said, beaming with pride. "Monkey meat!"

Roadkill Man's jaw dropped. "Are you *serious*?"

Mrs. Roadkill Man nodded. "Now, it's not perfect. The poor monkey accidentally fell into a trash compactor and, well . . . he got a little mutilated."

"Oh, honey, that doesn't matter," Roadkill Man said. "It's the *thought* that counts!"

Meanwhile, Amanda caught my eye and gestured at the kitchen clock. We were running out of time.

"Uh, I hate to bother you, Roadkill Man," I said. "But do you think we could have a word in private?"

CHAPTER

It wasn't easy to persuade Roadkill Man to let us use his prized mutilated monkey meat, but after we explained the whole thing to Mrs. Roadkill Man, she helped convince him.

"Aw, come on," Roadkill Man whined. "Can't I have just *a little* of the monkey myself?"

I sighed. "Okay, maybe. We'll have to see."

Roadkill Man grinned. It would have been a nice grin if he weren't missing so many teeth.

Amanda said she didn't think she could stomach making the mutilated monkey kebab, but luckily Mrs. Roadkill Man was glad to do it.

Meanwhile, dinner had ended and the orphan Sherpas cleared the dining hall. Then they set a table with a tablecloth, candles, plates, and silverware.

In the kitchen, Mrs. Roadkill Man hummed to herself as she cooked the monkey kebab. An orphan Sherpa stood near the kitchen door, peeking out every now and then to see if Brad had arrived.

Amanda sat near the door with her arms crossed and a glum look on her face. I knew she wasn't looking forward to eating dinner with Schmook the Crook.

"You sure you can go through with this?" I asked.

She shrugged. "I just feel so bad for that other monkey. Even if it isn't Fred."

"I think we ought to have a toast to the mutilated monkey," I said. I went to the cabinet and got out a bunch of glasses and filled them with grape juice. Everyone took one.

"Let's sing a song to cheer Amanda up," Justin said.

"Good idea," I said. Everyone nodded and we sang:

"Great green gobs of greasy grimy gopher guts
Mutilated monkey meat
Chopped-up birdy's feet
French-fried eyeballs rolling up and down the street
Oops! I forgot my spoon!"

"To the mutilated monkey!" I said, raising my glass. "A brave monkey who will serve this camp well."

"And will be well served," added Mrs. Roadkill Man, holding up the big frying pan with sizzling chunks of mutilated monkey in it.

"Brad is being here!" whispered the orphan

Sherpa who was watching the dining room.

We all tiptoed to the kitchen door and peaked out. Brad was standing in the dining room, looking down at the candlelit table. He was holding a bouquet of flowers in his hand.

"Aw, isn't that sweet?" Justin whispered. "He brought flowers!"

We backed away from the door.

"You ready?" I asked Amanda.

She nodded slowly.

I looked over at Mrs. Roadkill Man. "How's that monkey kebab doing?"

On the other side of the kitchen, Mrs. Roadkill Man had prepared a dinner plate. She picked up a small chunk of meat off the plate and popped it in her mouth. Then she licked her fingertips. "It's ready."

I turned back to Amanda. "Okay, this is it. Give it your best shot and don't forget: At the end of dinner you'll be dying for something sweet."

"At the end of dinner with Brad I'll be dying, period," Amanda cracked with half a smile.

Roadkill Man came over and handed Amanda the plate. "Listen, if there are any leftovers, I claim them."

Amanda gazed down sadly at the little chunks of brown meat. Her eyes started to glisten with tears. "I bet he was a nice little monkey, whoever he was."

For a second I thought she was going to burst into

tears. But she blinked them back. And took a deep breath.

"Ready?" I asked.

"Ready." She nodded.

I smiled back. "Go get him, tiger."

We watched from the kitchen as Amanda brought the plate of monkey kebab out to Brad.

"Uh, I brought these for you," he said, handing her the flowers.

"Oh, how sweet!" Amanda gushed as she took them.

Meanwhile, Brad sat down and stared hungrily at the plate. "Oh, man, shish kebab. I can't believe it!"

"Why don't you start eating," Amanda said. "I'll take these flowers into the kitchen and put them in some water."

Brad instantly started to wolf down the mutilated monkey kebab. Meanwhile, Amanda came back to the kitchen with the flowers. We all smiled and quietly traded high fives. Then we peeked out the doorway at Brad, who was still eating.

"Look at him stuff his face!" Justin whispered.

"If he only knew what he was eating," Amanda said.

It wasn't long before Brad had gulped down every morsel. Then he picked up the plate and held it to his face.

"He's licking the plate!" Justin whispered.

"Such lovely manners," I whispered with a grin.

Brad put down the plate. *Blurrrp!* He let out a loud belch and patted his stomach contentedly. Then he looked around as if for the first time noticing that Amanda wasn't there.

"You'd better get back out there," Justin whispered to her.

"Maybe he wants seconds," I added.

Amanda pushed through the kitchen doors and went back out. Brad smiled happily at her. "I was wondering where you went," he said. "That was the best shish kebab I ever had."

"I'm glad you liked it," Amanda replied.

Brad patted his stomach. *Urp!* He let out a little belch.

"Uh, you wouldn't happen to have any more, would you?" he asked.

"Let me check." Amanda took his plate and headed back toward the kitchen.

"She's coming back for seconds!" I called in a low voice over to Mrs. Roadkill Man.

But Roadkill Man shook his head and crossed his arms. "Nope. No way."

CHAPTER

38

"**W**hat do you mean?" I gasped. "Brad wants seconds."

"Forget it," Roadkill Man said. "He's not having any more monkey. You said I could have some, too."

"Aw, come on," Justin said. "What do you want cooked dead monkey meat for?"

"Because I'm tired of squashed squirrels, scraped skunks, demolished deer, rotten raccoon, and greasy gophers," Roadkill Man said. "I deserve a break today. And that means *monkey*! And *you* promised."

Mrs. Roadkill Man stood beside her husband and nodded in agreement. "It's only fair. After all, I did bring it back for him, not that Brad fellow."

"What's the problem?" Amanda asked as she came into the kitchen.

"Roadkill Man won't give up the rest of the mutilated monkey," Justin said. "He wants it for himself."

"Is there anything else in the animal hut that looks like it's not going to make it?" I asked.

Amanda thought for a moment. "Well, Benny the boa constrictor isn't doing very well. And Greg the guinea pig is on his last legs."

I turned back to Roadkill Man. "Okay, here's the deal. You give us the rest of the monkey kebab and I promise you'll get the boa constrictor and the guinea pig when they croak."

Roadkill Man thought it over. "What else do you have?"

I gave Amanda a look.

"Well, there's always the mice," Amanda said. "The new ones are born, and the old ones die all the time."

"Yum." Roadkill Man licked his lips and shared a look with his wife.

"I could make a lovely roasted rodent fondue, dear," she said.

Roadkill Man turned back to us. "Okay, throw in half a dozen dead mice and you've got a deal."

Amanda rolled her eyes and groaned. "I can't believe I'm agreeing to this."

"Great," I said, taking Brad's plate from Amanda and handing it to Mrs. Roadkill Man. "Pile it on."

A moment later we watched from the kitchen as Amanda brought a second helping of mutilated monkey kebab for Brad. She stood beside the table while Brad wolfed down the food.

"Gee, I've never seen anyone eat so much," Justin whispered. "He must be stuffed!"

"With dead monkey meat," I added with a smile.

Brad finished the second helping and leaned back in his chair. "Man, that was great!"

"You really liked it?" Amanda asked.

"Are you kidding?" Brad said. "It was — " Suddenly he stopped talking and frowned. "Hey, wait a minute! How come *you* didn't have any?"

Amanda blinked with surprise and shot a panicked glance back at the kitchen.

"Uh-oh!" Justin gasped. "I think we just got nailed!"

In the dining hall, Brad stared down at the empty plate with a frown and then looked at Amanda. "What's going on? There wasn't anything wrong with that shish kebab was there?"

"Uh, no, of course not," Amanda stammered.

"Then how come you didn't have any?" he demanded.

"Well . . . to tell you the truth, I did," Amanda said. "I was so hungry and it smelled so good that I had a whole bunch before you even got here." She paused and patted her stomach. "I'm as stuffed as you are."

"Oh, okay." Brad sat back and relaxed. "So, uh, now that we've eaten, want to go canoeing in the moonlight?"

"Why, I'd love to," Amanda said.

"Really?" Brad looked surprised. "Well, great. Let's go."

He started to get up.

"There's just one thing," Amanda said. "I still don't feel like the dinner is complete."

"Why not?" Brad asked.

"Because I have nothing for dessert," Amanda said. "Wouldn't you just love something sweet right now?"

"You know, you're right," Brad said.

"Too bad there's nothing sweet in this whole camp," Amanda said. "I mean, you couldn't even have toothpaste for dessert. The campers have eaten all of it."

Brad nodded.

"I guess that's life," Amanda said with a shrug. She looked pretty bummed.

"Would having something sweet really make you happy?" Brad asked.

"Don't tease me," Amanda said. "You know there's nothing sweet for miles."

"Well, just suppose," Brad said. "Suppose I could find something sweet. Would it be worth a kiss?"

"What a slimeball!" Justin gasped in the kitchen.

"You mean on the cheek, right?" Amanda replied.

Brad nodded.

"Something sweet like what?" Amanda asked, pretending to act suspicious.

"Oh, I don't know," Brad said with a smile. "A Hershey's bar? Three Musketeers? M&M's?"

"Are you serious?" Amanda gasped.

"Would it be worth a kiss on the cheek?" Brad asked again.

"Oh, definitely," Amanda said.

Brad grinned. "Don't go anywhere. I'll be right back."

In the kitchen I spun around to Bag. "He fell for it! Send out the orphan Sherpas to follow him. We have to know *exactly* where he goes for the candy."

"Your wish is being my command," Bag replied. Then he turned to the orphan Sherpas and whispered some orders in Tibetan. The orphan Sherpas quickly filed out the back door of the kitchen and disappeared into the dark.

"You think they'll be able to follow Brad without him noticing?" Justin asked nervously.

"The Sherpas are being the best trackers in the world," Bag replied. "This Brad Schmook will never know they are following him."

It wasn't long before Brad returned to the dining hall. He reached into his pocket and pulled out two candy bars and a box of M&M's. "Surprise," he said with a smile.

"Oh, Brad! I can't believe it!" Amanda gasped.

At the same time, an orphan Sherpa hurried into the kitchen and whispered something to Bag.

"What'd he say?" Justin asked.

"He said the candy is being hidden in the golf shack," Bag reported. "He said he has seen many boxes of candy being inside."

"That's it!" Justin gasped.

Slap! He and I shared a high five.

Meanwhile, out in the dining hall Brad stepped close to Amanda. "Now, how about that kiss on the cheek?" He closed his eyes and stuck his face toward her.

Amanda looked back at the kitchen. I pushed open the door and gave her the thumbs-up sign.

Amanda turned back to Brad, who was still standing there with his eyes closed. She pulled back her fist.

Pow! She punched him right in the nose.

Thwamp! Brad fell backwards to the floor and grabbed his nose. Meanwhile, Justin and I came out of the kitchen and joined Amanda.

"Hey! What'd you do *that* for?" Brad cried.

"She did it because you stole all the candy and then tried to get rich off the campers by selling it to them at ridiculous prices," I said.

Brad stared up at us. "You tricked me!"

"Not as bad as you tricked all the campers and stole their money," Justin said.

Still holding his nose, Brad got to his feet. "You may think you've won, but you haven't. You don't know where the candy is. Only I know, and I'll *never* tell."

"It's in the golf shack," I said.

Brad's jaw dropped with surprise. "How did you find out?"

"We had you followed," Justin said.

"Well, I'm gonna tell Mr. Kirby," Brad said. "The golf course is strictly off-limits to everyone from Camp Run-a-Muck. You're not allowed near it."

"Fine," I said. "And while you're telling him that, you might want to tell him what you had for dinner."

Brad frowned. "He doesn't care if I have shish kebab."

"Maybe not," Justin said. "But you should."

"Why?" Brad asked.

"Because it was made from mutilated monkey meat," I said.

"Liar," Brad said.

"Go look in the kitchen," I said. "There's a big woman and longhaired hippie guy in there. I'm sure they'll be glad to show you the parts they didn't cook."

"Like the paws and tail," Justin added.

Brad rushed toward the kitchen and pushed through the doors.

"*Ahhhhhhhhhhhhhh!*" A moment later we heard a scream.

"I guess Brad believes us now," Justin said with a smile.

CHAPTER

41

While Brad barfed his brains out, the rest of us went to the golf shack and got all the candy. Then we went from cabin to cabin all through camp, giving it away for free.

"Free candy!" Ralphie gasped when Justin gave him a Three Musketeers. "Did you really say 'free'?"

"Believe it," Justin said. "And take some Sugar Babies, too."

Everywhere we went, kids ran around, stuffing their faces with candy and screaming for joy. Camp Run-a-Muck was starting to be a happy place again.

"I can't believe this!" Ricky Pulger cried as he chewed on a mouthful of M&M's. "It's a miracle!"

"Kind of makes you feel like Robin Hood," Justin said after we gave away the last of the candy. Not far away, Roadkill Man and his wife were walking toward the forest. Roadkill Man was carrying the sack containing the new forms of roadkill his wife had found.

"Where are you going?" I asked.

"Back to the cave," Roadkill Man replied. "To cook up the rest of these goodies."

We waved good-bye. All around us, the camp was in an uproar as kids dashed around laughing and playing.

"Let's go down to the waterfront," I said. "At least it'll be quiet there."

Soon we were walking along the dock. The sun had gone down. Above us the stars were starting to come out.

"I just hope wherever that poor mutilated monkey is right now, he doesn't mind too much," Amanda said with a sigh as she gazed up at the sky.

"I'm sure he's in monkey heaven," I said, watching the small waves lap against the dock.

"Hey, that reminds me of a joke," said Justin.

"So what else is new?" I asked with a sigh.

"How did the man get to heaven?" Justin asked.

"I don't know, Justin, how?" I said.

"Flu." Justin grinned.

Amanda and I shared a look.

"You thinking what I'm thinking?" I asked.

"Definitely," said Amanda.

We each put a hand on Justin's shoulder.

And pushed.

Ker-splash!

About the Author

Todd Strasser has written many award-winning novels for young and teenage readers. Among his best-known are *Help! I'm Trapped in Obedience School* and *The Diving Bell*. He speaks frequently at schools about the craft of writing and conducts writing workshops for young people. He and his family live outside New York City with their yellow Labrador retriever, Mac.

IT'S A GUT-BUSTING GROSS-OUT!

CAMP RUN-A-MUCK #1

TODD STRASSER

YOU NEED *GUTS* TO EAT HERE!

When Justin and Lucas snag summer jobs as assistant cooks at Camp Run-a-Muck, there's only one problem: They have no idea how to cook! But when the despicable Camp Director Bob "The Blob" Kirby hogs the best food for his own private bar-b-que, the duo create *their* own recipe for revenge: Switch the hamburger meat for The Blob's cookout with ground-up dead gopher meat!

Camp Run-a-Muck #1:
Greasy Grimy Gopher Guts

DON'T MISS
#2 Mutilated Monkey Meat
#3 Chopped Up Birdy's Feet

CRA11196

IT'S A GUT-BUSTING GROSS-OUT!

CAMP RUN-A-MUCK #3

TODD STRASSER

A PERFECT 10 ON THE BARF-O-METER!

No matter how bad Camp Run-a-Muck gets, it's still fun. But Camp director Bob "The Blob" Kirby wants to sell it, or turn it into a golf resort. Justin and Lucas know there's only one way out: to win the Defungo Deodorant Million Dollar Hole-In-One contest. And believe it or not, Roadkill Man is a pretty good golfer (not to mention their only hope)! Can the gang save Camp Run-a-Muck?

Camp Run-a-Muck #3: Chopped Up Birdy's Feet

DON'T MISS

#1 Greasy Grimy Gopher Guts
#2 Mutilated Monkey Meat

CRA31196